Buster the Biker Sheep

Rob Portlock

INTERVARSITY PRESS
DOWNERS GROVE, ILLINOIS 60515

All rights reserved. No part of this book may be reproduced in any form without written permission from InterVarsity Press, P.O. Box 1400, Downers Grove, Illinois 60515.

InterVarsity Press® is the book-publishing division of InterVarsity Christian Fellowship®, a student movement active on campus at hundreds of universities, colleges and schools of nursing in the United States of America, and a member movement of the International Fellowship of Evangelical Students. For information about local and regional activities, write Public Relations Dept., InterVarsity Christian Fellowship, 6400 Schroeder Rd., P.O. Box 7895, Madison, WI 53707-7895.

All Scripture quotations, unless otherwise indicated, are taken from the HOLY BIBLE, NEW INTERNATIONAL VERSION®. NIV®. Copyright© 1973, 1978, 1984 by International Bible Society. Used by permission of Zondervan Publishing House. All rights reserved.

Cover illustration: Rob Portlock

ISBN 0-8308-1904-5

Printed in Mexico

Library of Congress Cataloging-in-Publication Data has been requested.

15	14	13	12	11	10	9	8	7	6	5	4	3	2	1
05	04	03	02	01	00	99	98	97	96	95	94	93		

With gratitude
to Paul & Anne Leavens,
the real Woolsleys,
and to
the Sunday Night Gang

I love to spend the evening at Mr. and Mrs. Woolsley's house. Their house is the best place to visit.

Every Sunday night they have a study about what it is like to have a Shepherd.

Every week is the same. We all walk to the Woolsleys' house together. (Well, all of us except Buster and his friends. Buster never wants to come.)

The Woolsleys greet us at the door with a hug as though they had not seen us for a year.

We sit together on the floor. The Woolsleys tell us about the Shepherd.

None of us have seen the Shepherd. But from the way they talk, we know he is real.

Sometimes while they are telling us stories, I think I see Buster's face peeking in the window. But I can never quite catch him.

Soon the study is over. We have to wait until the next week to hear more about the Shepherd.

Around town, Buster and his friends talk about us.

One day, Buster said to me, "I don't believe there's a Shepherd. You guys are just dumb!"

Then I said, "There *is* a Shepherd. I believe it in my heart."

Buster said, "Well, have you ever seen him? Huh? Have you ever heard his voice?"

"No," I said. "But I know one day I will, and I will be ready to follow him!"

"Well, you can go ahead and waste your time. I've got better things to do!" said Buster as he walked away.

"Wait! Wait!" I cried. "Come with me to meet the sheep that have seen him and heard his voice."

Buster said, "You are crazy! You've been sheared one too many times."

I just shook my head sadly.

Later that week we went to the meadow. We were all drinking water. Willie suddenly froze. He looked up at the mountains. "Did you hear that?"

"Yes," said Samantha.

"I heard it," yelled Fred.

"Me too!" Maria said.

"Wow!" said Denise.

"Did you hear him say, 'Come with me'?" asked Larry excitedly.

I said, "I'm going to tell Buster!"

We ran to tell Buster the good news.

"We heard him. We heard the Shepherd," we squealed.

"I was standing right behind you in the trees. I didn't hear anything," Buster replied.

We ran down the street telling all the other sheep about the wonderful voice we had heard.

That Saturday we decided to go up on the mountain and pick wildflowers to give to Mr. and Mrs. Woolsley.

We picked the flowers, and we played. We were rolling in the flowers when Buddy suddenly stopped. He pointed and said, "Look. It's him!"

We all looked. On the ridge we saw him. As soon as we saw him, he was gone.

We began to jump with joy. "It's true. It's true," we sang. "There is a Shepherd."

We could not wait to tell the Woolsleys the good news.

On Sunday, we all started out for the Shepherd study. But we couldn't find Buster.

Then, as we were walking on the path, we saw Buster leaning against a tree.

Buster said, "I hope you're not going to that Shepherd study." Pointing to the woods, he said, "I know there are wolves out there. You better go back!"

"We can't go back now. We have seen the Shepherd," said Wendy. "Even if there are wolves, he will protect us."

So on we went.

Buster headed back to town. As he walked through the woods, he laughed about the wolf story he had told the other sheep.

Suddenly, he heard a noise. Buster slowed down. Then he saw a shadow. Buster started shaking. Out from behind a tree stepped a giant wolf.

The wolf looked at Buster and said, "Glad to see you. My stomach has been growling."

The wolf stepped toward him. Now Buster was backed up against a tree.

"Please, Mr. Wolf, I just want to go home!" he said.

"Your next home will be in my belly!" said the wolf, and he reached out to grab Buster.

Buster screamed, *"Shepherd, help me!"*

The wolf froze and looked over his shoulder. There, in the distance, stood the Shepherd. The wolf said, "I had better be going." With that he disappeared into the trees.

We arrived at the house with joyful hearts and told the Woolsleys of all we had heard and seen.

The Woolsleys said, "Tonight is the night. If we are still, he will come."

At that moment Buster came through the door, wide-eyed and trembling.

"I believe now!" he shouted. "I have seen him and heard him, and he is here."

We rushed to the window.
There in the field stood the Shepherd.

As we turned around, the Woolsleys said, "Little sheep, we have taught you everything that we can. It is time to go and learn from the Shepherd himself."

We hugged the Woolsleys goodby and merrily joined the Shepherd's flock.

How to Talk to a Child About This Book

Most children will not recognize the symbolism of the Shepherd as Christ without some help. Talk to them about how Christ is a Shepherd who cares for us—the sheep. And talk about their fears and how they would like to be protected. Help them to understand how they can call on the Shepherd when they are worried or afraid. Read Psalm 23:1-4 together:

> The LORD is my shepherd, I shall not be in want.
>> He makes me lie down in green pastures,
> he leads me beside quiet waters,
>> he restores my soul.
> He guides me in paths of righteousness
>> for his name's sake.
> Even though I walk
>> through the valley of the shadow of death,
> I will fear no evil,
>> for you are with me;
> your rod and your staff,
>> they comfort me.

You may want to look up the passage in a children's Bible and read it there. Talk together about what these verses mean to you, and how God offers you comfort.

The Publisher